Babar and the Crocodile

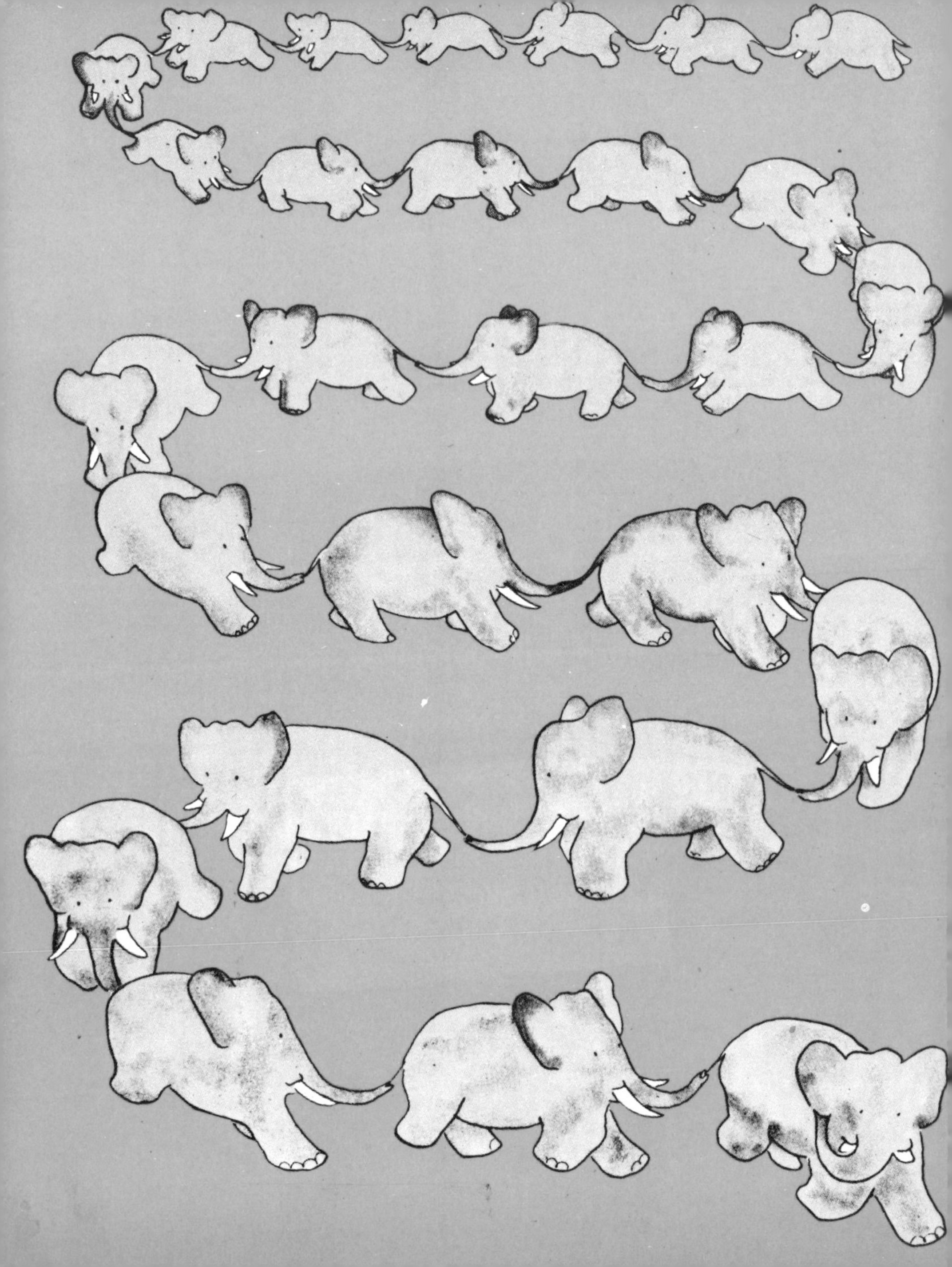

JEAN DE BRUNHOFF

BABAR AND THE CROCODILE

A MAGNET BOOK

Pom, Flora and Alexander,
the children of King Babar and Queen Celeste,
were out for a walk
in their big perambulator,
pushed by their cousin Arthur.
"Faster!" demanded Alexander.
Arthur, who was going carefully,
avoiding the stones,
began to run, let go the handle,
caught it again, and ran on.
The children thought this great fun.

Hearing the nurse coming,
Arthur turned his head for a moment.
He let go the handle, and the pram
began to roll away by itself down a slope.
Arthur ran after it as hard as he could.
The nurse ran too. A little lower down
the road turned and ran along the side
of a deep ravine. The pram was in great danger!
Martha the tortoise, who was walking nearby,
ran as fast as her little legs could go.

She threw herself in front of the wheels just as the pram was about to fall over the precipice. Pom and Flora were caught by the hood, but poor Alexander was shot out.

Fortunately
Alexander managed to hold on
to the branch of a tree.
Some squirrels had seen the acciden
and leapt to help.
"Courage, little elephant!
Don't let go!
We are coming!
Try to put your foot
on the thick branch."

The plan having succeeded,
Mr Squirrel gave instructions:
"Hold tight to my tail,
and, to balance yourself,
wave your great big ears about.
Take care! Follow me.
You shall have a rest
when you are safe
in our house."
A few moments later
Alexander was safe.

The squirrels asked the giraffe to carry Alexander home. Soon she put him gently into Babar's outstretched trunk.

Some months later
Babar decided to arrange a picnic.
He had promised the children this for some time.
The day came, the weather was glorious,
the family in high spirits.
Zephir led the party.
A gentle little donkey
carried the picnic baskets
on its back.
Pom, Flora and Alexander
sat on top.
Cornelius got very hot,
but managed to keep up.

After a long walk,
hungry and tired, they gladly settled
down in a beautiful green field
not far from the river.
They all ate a delicious lunch.
The air was fresh, the sun shone.
If the ants had been
less greedy
all would have been perfect.

After lunch Celeste put away the plates.
Arthur and Zephir collected up the scattered paper.
Babar went fishing in the river nearby,
and Cornelius stretched himself out for a nap.
He took off his bowler hat and put it
beside him. He put a handkerchief
on his head to stop
the flies from settling there,
and fell into a deep sleep.
Alexander looked at him
and beckoned to Pom and Flora.

Alexander lifted Cornelius' hat.
Creeping underneath it,
he walked about, taking very small steps.
"What a funny tortoise!"
said Pom, laughing.
Playing about,
they reached the river bank,
and then Alexander had another idea . . .

He put the hat in the water. "What a fine boat!"

he said, and got into it. It floated! It was wonderful!

Suddenly Alexander noticed
a crocodile coming
very swiftly towards him.
"Oh! Papa!" he screamed.
Babar was fishing peacefully,
and thought that the children were playing
happily, but this little frightened cry
made him leap up.

Babar roared with anger
when he saw that old rogue the crocodile.
Three seconds in which to act,
and he had no gun!
The situation was desperate!
Babar, without a moment's hesitation,
seized the anchor of the boat
and threw it with all his might
into the jaws of the monster,
while Alexander crouched down in the hat.

The crocodile, hooked like a little fish,
swished his tail furiously.
The hat, drawn into the eddy, sank,
and Alexander fell into the water.

Babar dived in and groped about with his trunk.
He felt something!
Thank goodness! It was Alexander's ear!
He pulled him to the surface.

Alexander had had a bad fright.
Babar took him quickly back to his mother
and to put on dry clothes.
Poor Alexander!

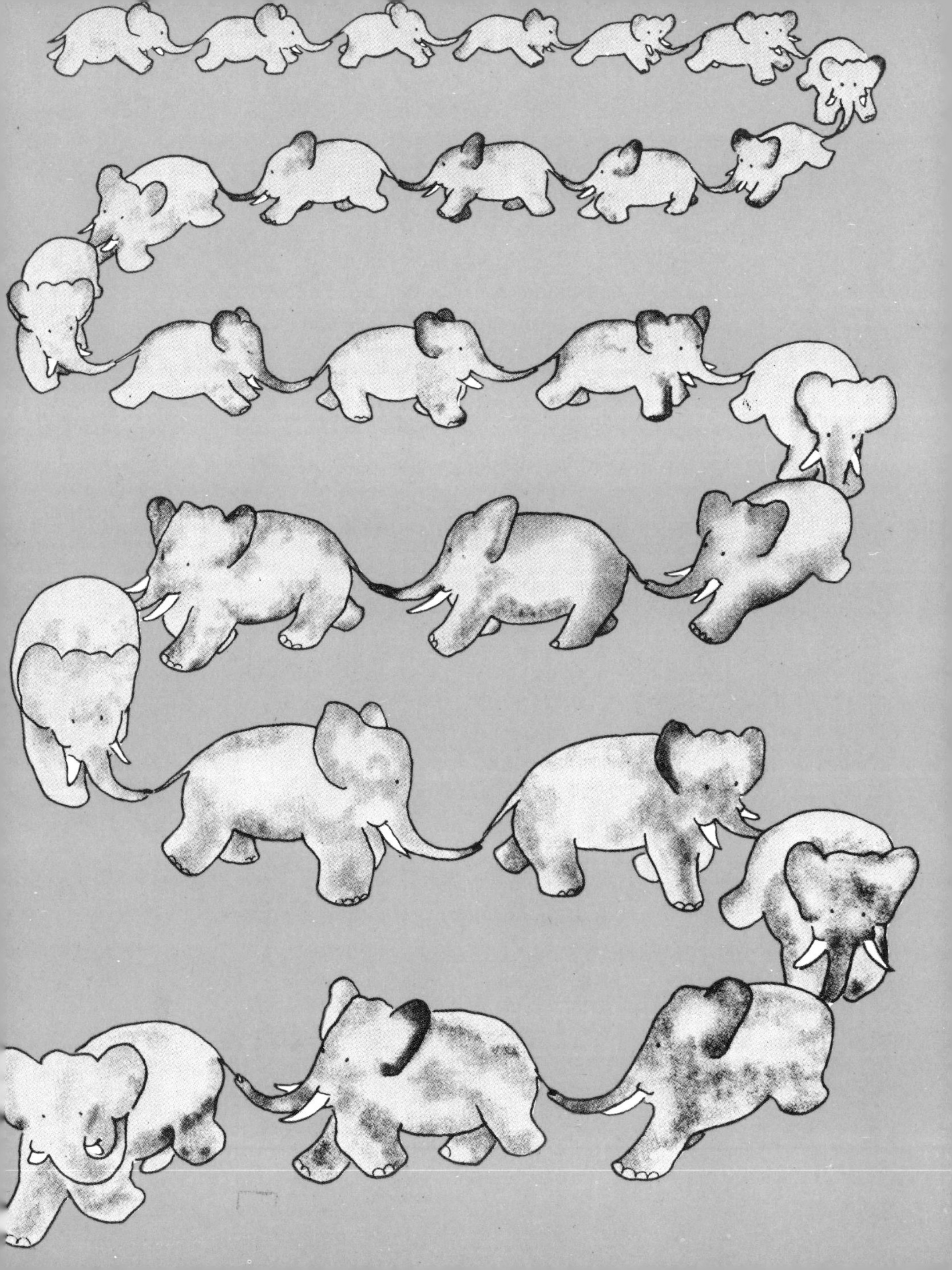

First published in Great Britain 1970
by Methuen & Co Ltd
First published by Librairie Hachette as *Babar et le Crocodile*
Magnet edition first published 1979
by Methuen Children's Books Ltd
11 New Fetter Lane, London EC4P 4EE
Reprinted 1979

Printed in Great Britain by
Fakenham Press Limited, Fakenham, Norfolk
ISBN 0 416 88180 7